HAPPY LITTLE SUN

ZHILU ZHANG · MING EN

Every morning, a happy
Little Sun jumped out of the sea.

Little Sun sang a song while rising
slowly behind the mountains.

That's when all the animals of
the mountains woke up.

One day, Little Sun said,
"Hi, everyone. What game
should we play today?"

"How about racing?"
said Gray Rabbit.

"Great!" said
Little Sun.

Gray Rabbit ran to the west
as fast as he could.

He
ran

and ran.

He jumped over a creek

and dashed up a hill.

Out of breath, he looked up and found **Little Sun** smiling at him from just above his head.

Upset that he lost the race, Gray Rabbit went back to his rabbit hole.

The next day,
Little Sun asked again,

"Hi everyone. What
should we play
today?"

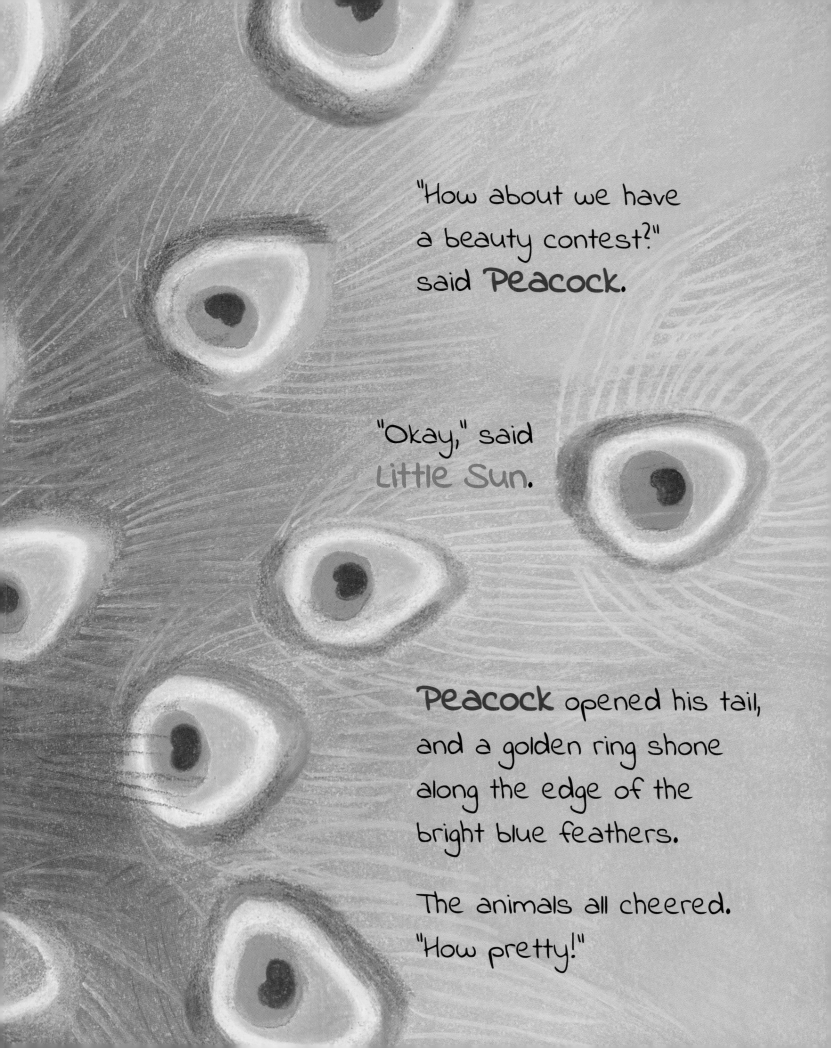

"How about we have
a beauty contest?"
said Peacock.

"Okay," said
Little Sun.

Peacock opened his tail,
and a golden ring shone
along the edge of the
bright blue feathers.

The animals all cheered.
"How pretty!"

Little Sun smiled confidently and cast his rays through the water droplets in the air.

A beautiful
rainbow
with all seven colors
appeared in the sky.

"That's prettier!"

cheered the animals.

Embarrassed,
Peacock closed
his tail.

"What is the
next game?"
Little Sun said,
loudly and proudly.

"How about hide-and-seek?"
a **deep voice** whispered.

"Who are you?" Little Sun asked.

"Where are you?" asked Little Sun.

"I am on the west side of this big banyan tree," said the deep voice.

"I am coming to find you,"
Little Sun said.

Little Sun went to the west of the banyan tree but didn't find **Shade**.

"Where are you?"
Little Sun asked impatiently.

"I am now on the east side of the banyan tree," Shade said with a smile.

Little Sun could not go backward,
no matter how impatient he got.

"Just wait and see," said Little Sun.
"I will surely catch you tomorrow."

"Okay. See you
tomorrow," said Shade.

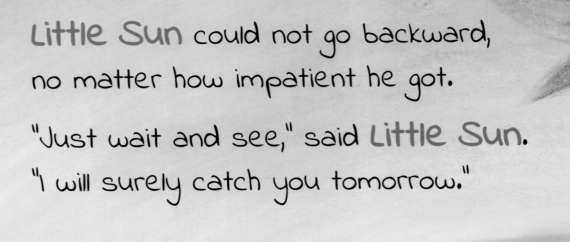

The next morning, Little Sun shouted immediately after he made his way above the mountains,

"Shade, are you up?"

Shade answered, "Sure. I am up when you are."

"Where are you hiding this time?" Little Sun asked."

On the west side of the banyan tree," Shade answered.

"You'd better not lie to me," said Little Sun.

"Yes, yes, we all see **Shade**," said Gray Rabbit and **Peacock**.

"He is on the west side of the banyan tree."

"I am coming!"

Little Sun said.

Little Sun went higher and higher.

He was now above the top of the banyan tree.

But he didn't see Shade.

"Peacock, do you see Shade?"
Little Sun asked.

"Yes. I am resting with Shade,"
Peacock answered.

Little Sun arrived at the west side of the banyan tree and searched and searched.

He heard Shade laugh. "Now I am on the east side of the banyan tree."

"That's right! we all see him!"
Gray Rabbit and Peacock
said, loudly and proudly.

Disappointed, Little Sun
stopped his search.
No matter how hard he tried,
he could not find Shade.

Do you know why?

ZHILU ZHANG

Zhilu Zhang is the deputy director of the China writer's Association children's literature committee. When he's not writing children's books he writes screenplays for China's Film Group Corporation and has won multiple international film awards.

MING EN

Ming En is an award-winning illustrator of picture books and children's magazines. She serves as Art Director at China Children's Publication and Press Group.

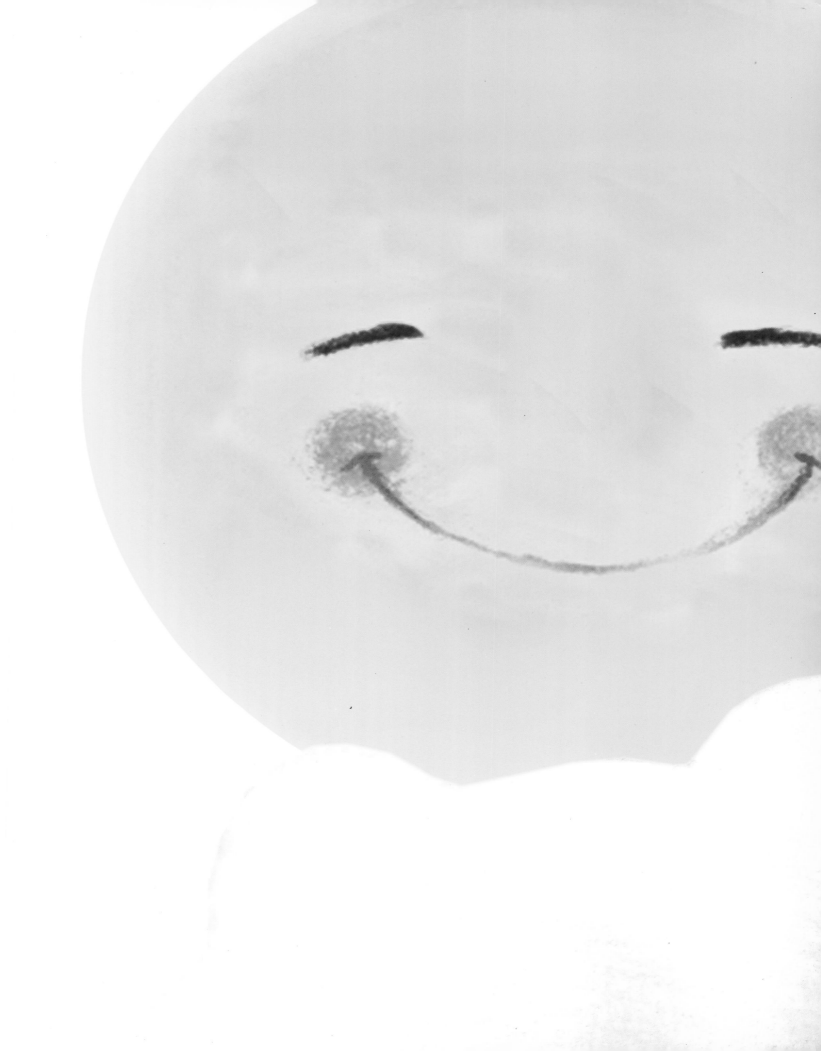

US $9.95

ISBN: 978-1-4788-6916-0

9 781478 869160

50995